Colin Ridyard
Illustrations by Sonia Sparkles

Eddie the Elephant and the Pirate Treasure

Nightingale Books

NIGHTINGALE PAPERBACK

A CIP catalogue record for this title is
available from the British Library.
ISBN 978-1-83875-368-9

Nightingale Books is an imprint of
Pegasus Elliot MacKenzie Publishers Ltd.
www.pegasuspublishers.com

First Published in 2021

Nightingale Books
Sheraton House Castle Park
Cambridge England

Printed & Bound in Great Britain

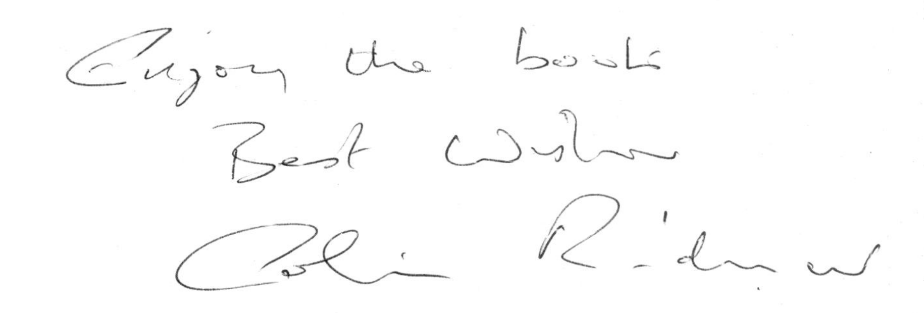

About the Author

Colin Ridyard, the author, lives in Wales with his family and works as an academic researcher and occasionally as a teacher too.

Eddie the Elephant and the Pirate Treasure

Disclaimer

Remember, parents, Eddie is a particularly well-behaved talking elephant and generally speaking, taking wild elephants to children's parties is not something to be recommended. The characters, locations and events portrayed in this book exist purely in the imagination of the reader, which means they are in fact, very, very real, indeed. However, any similarity to people, living or dead or yet to be born; or events, past, present or future, are entirely coincidental and not intended by the author.

Dedication

This book is dedicated to the treasured memory of Sensei Ayman Al-Hameed, my dearest friend, brother, mentor and confidant.

26

Once there was a girl called Jackie who lived in a house at number twenty-six, Stamford Drive with her mummy and daddy.

Jackie had a lot of friends. They included: the fireman's twins Billy and Jane, Sian the ironmongers' daughter, Angus whose daddy worked in the bank and Rani whose daddy painted pictures. She also had one extra special friend who was quite unusual as far as friends go because he had big floppy ears, a long trunk, and a HUGE appetite. His name was Eddie the Elephant!

You are invited to Rani's
Beach Party at Bakewell's beach
on Saturday 16th July 11am

It was the first day of the summer holidays and to celebrate the end of school the children had arranged a party on nearby Bakewell Beach.

"Ooooh!" squealed Eddie the elephant happily, reading the invite. "There'll be jam tarts, buns, apples, cheese sandwiches, pizza, ice cream and orange juice..."

"...And an extra strong, industrial strength, elephant-proof bouncy castle," laughed Daddy remembering what happened the last time Eddie played on a trampoline.

"Everyone into the car then," said Mummy grinning from ear to ear.

"Eddie, you'd best sit in the front of the car next to me," said Daddy. "Mummy, you can sit behind me — that way, the weight will be more evenly distributed."

Off they drove, with Eddie's trunk sticking out of the side window waving merrily. "Wheeeeeeee!" he laughed.

"You should have gone before we left," Daddy grumbled.

There was only one slight problem driving with an elephant in the front of the car... drivers coming in the opposite direction.

SCREEEEEEEEEEECCCCHHHHHHHHH!

Fortunately, there were no 'bumps' or 'badoinnngggs'.

"I love the way their eyes open up so wide and how they stare," laughed Eddie.

"They should keep their eyes on the road!" Daddy said disapprovingly.

"I think Eddie had better wear a disguise," said Mummy. "Here, put on these sunglasses, fold your ears back with this headband and for goodness' sake, roll your trunk in!"

"OK," said Eddie, his cheeks turning bright red.

"Are we there yet?" Jackie asked after half an hour.

"No," said Daddy. "Still a way to go."

"Are we there yet?" Eddie asked ten minutes later.

"No!" Mummy replied. "Not yet."

"Are we there yet?" asked Jackie and Eddie together five minutes later.

"NO!" said Mummy and Daddy together.

Pretty soon, however, the seaside came into view.

"Hooray!" said Eddie and Jackie together. But just then a huge rain cloud blotted out the sun and...

Splish! Splash! Splosh!

"Oh dear," said Daddy, turning on the windscreen wipers.

"Never mind," said Mummy. "It won't last long, and we can visit the Bakewell Beach Museum while we're waiting for the sun to come back out."

The museum was full of amazing things: a model dinosaur fish, a huge trilobite fossil, some actors dressed as smugglers AND a large pirate boat! On the wall was a painting of the meanest-looking pirate Jackie had ever seen.

"Who was he?" she asked.

"That was Henry Slade," Daddy replied. "The richest pirate who ever sailed the seven seas. He lived on Bakewell Beach and some people say he buried all his treasure in the sand here."

"But no one has ever found it," Mummy added.

"Ooooh!" said Eddie, his eyes shining. "Can we go and look for it? If I found the treasure I would be very rich, and I could buy a big house for my mummy and daddy and they wouldn't have to live in a zoo anymore."

"It's only a story," said Mummy, patting Eddie on the shoulder. "Oh look!" she added, pointing at the window. "The rain has stopped – ice cream, anyone?"

"Yes please," said Jackie, Eddie and Daddy all at the same time.

Outside the sun was shining brightly and the waves from the glistening sea lapped lazily on the sand. The smell of fried onions and candy floss wafted on the warm wind and the tap, tap, bang, bang of people building sandcastles and the flap, flap of deckchairs filled the air.

"Ice cream for the little elephant," called a friendly seller's voice and a minute later Eddie had the biggest ice cream a little elephant had ever seen. Suddenly, a sneaky seagull swooped past and painfully pecked Eddie on the trunk making him drop it!

"Ow! Ow! Ow!" wailed Eddie, big tears streaming down his cheeks and holding his trunk which truth be told is a very sensitive spot for a baby elephant.

"Wark! Wark! Wark!" chorused a gang of seagulls crowding round Eddie's dropped ice cream and gobbling it up. He tried to shoo them away, but they just pecked at him.

"Oh fiddlesticks," said Mummy.

"Fiddlesticks are inanimate objects," Eddie snorted, still shooing the seagulls away. "These horrid birds are definitely animate, they're also cheeky, sneaky and bothersomely beaky!"

"Never mind," said Jackie, giving Eddie a big hug and handing him her ice cream. "You can have mine."

Just then, an enormous crab grabbed the ice cream in a claw and scuttled away.

"Come back!" shouted Eddie chasing after the ice cream thief.

The crab stopped, turned around and nipped poor Eddie in the trunk with its other claw. "Ow! Ow! Ow!" wailed Eddie, more big tears streaming down his cheeks.

"Oh dear," said Daddy.

"He's not a deer," snorted Eddie, still holding his trunk. "Deers are cute and lovable. Dis horrid crab is all snippy, grippy and nastily nippy!"

"Never mind," said Jackie, putting some ointment on his trunk. "Let's dig for the pirate treasure instead."

They dug and they dug and they dug. Soon the beach was covered in holes. Big holes, little holes, round holes, square holes and a ginormous hole placed in a rather precarious position!

"YEEEEEOWWWWWWWWW!"

There was a big spladumph! Two seconds later, a man climbed out of the hole with ice cream cones stuck to each ear. He looked like a crimson-cheeked cow.

"Somebody prevent that pesky pachyderm from digging holes," he shouted.

"Oh dear," said Mummy and Daddy together. "Come along children, it's nearly time for the beach party to start!"

It did not take them long to find the party.

"Hey! Jackie! Eddie!" came a chorus of voices. It was Billy, Jane, Angus, Sian and Rani and they were bouncing up and down on the biggest bouncy castle Jackie had ever seen.

"Bouncy castles!" squealed Eddie excitedly. "I love bouncy castles!" And before anyone could hold him back, Eddie had run up to the bouncy castle and jumped on it. He bounced so hard he flew off towards the sea!

SPLADOOOOOOSH!

"I've never seen an elephant fly before!" chuckled one cheeky codfish.

"Perhaps he's a new kind of jumbo jet!" chortled another. "And look! He hasn't got any swimming trunks!"

"That's because us elephants already have trunks!" said Eddie indignantly. He turned around and swam back to the shore.

"Try and be a bit more careful this time," said Daddy as Eddie very carefully got on to the bouncy castle again.

KERBOING! Eddie did angel wings with his ears! KERBOING-G-G! He bounced higher and did a starfish with his arms, legs, and trunk! KERBOING-G-G-G-G! He did a double pike and somersault (which quite frankly for a baby elephant is quite an achievement) and then,

KERBOING-G-G-G-G! SPLADOOOMPH!

Missing the bouncy castle completely, poor Eddie landed on the sand and left a huge elephant-shaped hole!

"Oh dear," cried everyone in unison.

"Eddie, are you OK?" asked Mummy with her hands near her mouth.

"Ow! Ow! Ow!" said Eddie. "There's something hard down here!"

"Be careful down there," called Daddy. "It might be an old wartime bomb."

"I don't think so," Eddie called back. "It's made out of wood with bits of metal."

"It might be an old, buried boat," suggested Mummy.

"Too small," said Eddie. "Hold on, I've loosened it. I'm bringing it up now!"

Eddie emerged from the hole with a huge wooden chest studded with metal rivets. He opened it up and inside were shiny, sparkly rubies, diamonds and emeralds embedded in rings, bracelets, necklaces and tiaras.

"The pirate's treasure," said Jackie, her blue eyes sparkling brighter than the glittering sea. The children and Eddie all put the trinkets on and started dancing around.

"Hooray," laughed Rani. "We all look like princes and princesses now!"

"Better put them back in the chest," said Daddy.

The children did as they were told.

"But why?" asked Eddie.

"When we find treasure like this we must hand it to the police station over there," said Daddy pointing in the direction of Bakewell town. "But we will get a big reward."

Everyone looked where he was pointing and started chatting about how nice it would be to get a reward. But when they turned to look at the treasure again it was gone! Nasty Nobby the naughty thief had pinched it and was sailing away in the pirate ship which he'd pinched from the museum.

"Stop, thief!" shouted Mummy.

"No chance," laughed Nobby. "I'll get a lot of money for these in Spitalfields market!" He didn't laugh long though! SPLADOOOSHHHHHHH!

In a matter of seconds, Eddie ran at the bouncy castle like he had done before, bounced high in the air and dive bombed the pirate ship. He hit the boat so hard it made the thief go flying head over heels and left him upside down with his underpants flying from the pirate ship flag post instead of the Jolly Roger.

Three minutes later, a police car came and took Nasty Nobby the naughty thief to jail.

"Thank you so much, Eddie," said Jackie.

"Yes, well done," said Angus.

"You'll be able to buy that house now, Eddie," said Mummy and Daddy together.

So, if you are ever in Stamford Drive do pop round to number twenty-six because next door at number twenty-five there is a house full of elephants who invite lots of other zoo animals over to stay on holiday. Would you like to have elephants as neighbours? I know I would, especially if one of them was Eddie the Elephant.